HARDCASTLE BOOKS

The Untouchable Sky

A TALE OF ELSEWHEN

THE JAIME SKYE CHRONICLES
BOOK 0

WILL FORREST

ISBN: 978-1-990115-82-0

1st edition 2023

Content Note:

Please be aware this book includes references to medical trauma,
parental death, and attempted suicide.

THE UNTOUCHABLE SKY

AN ORDINARY MAN

Jamie Skye was finally ordinary. It had taken all his life, untold hours in doctors' surgeries, unremembered weeks in hospitals and sanatoriums, and more than once a visit to a college lecture hall where he was not a student but the subject of the lecture. At last, at the age of thirty-four, he could safely say that he had become wholly unremarkable, and wished only to remain so for the rest of his life.

Which is why when the extraordinary man walked in, Jaime at once lowered his eyes and did not look up again until the man's mellifluous voice disappeared behind Corporal Brigg's door. It being nearly ten in the morning he was of course the only one in the patent office, Pickford out on a call and Tyburn likely still face down under a pile of his own faded excuses.

But that was none of Jaime's business. He had steady employment at an undemanding post in a minor division of civil service, and if he spent more time than was perhaps appropriate on his drunken colleague's cases instead of his own, it was all in the name of the public good. Not only that, but if Tyburn were sacked it would likely kill him, as the only time he wasn't at least half-cut was at work.

Jaime would have smelled it if he was, that sickly taint in the air round a drunk, exuded from their breath, from their very skin. Morally Jaime was indifferent to alcohol and those who drank it, believing one made one's own peace with one's creator, but his un-ordinariness included being too sensitive to strange aromas, so that speaking to Tyburn was an act of courage, a prolonged conversation cause for a strong cup of tea.

Tyburn wasn't here, and neither was his polar opposite Pickford, whose specialty was machines too large or complicated to be brought to the office, and whose pernickety habit was to be at the hapless patent-seeker's establishment at first light. Jaime liked the office on such mornings, with no sound but the scratch of his pen nib and the squeak of the wheels on his chair, the sunlight casting little rainbows everywhere through the strips of stained glass atop the southeast facing windows.

The stranger's aroma of gunpowder and lilacs lingered in the unstirred air, making Jaime's nose itch as he pored over an engraving of a 'device for improving the application of whitewash.' The scent matched the man, or what Jaime had seen of him before deciding rightfully to ignore him. Matched his scarlet coat and the lace at his wrists and his unfashionably long hair and his mellifluous voice which Jaime had heard for scant seconds and so therefore should not be able to hear in his mind as clearly as if the man stood before him.

"Who are you?"

Jaime stayed as he was, his eye pressed to a magnifying loupe held three inches from the intricate diagram. "No one important."

"Lord Lear, this is Skye," said Corporal Brigg.

Lord Lear. Jaime put aside the loupe and sat upright. The man was even more extraordinary close up, with a sharp face and eyes so darkly brown they were nearly black, though his irises were rimmed with green.

"Stand up, Skye, and account for yourself," Brigg said through his yellowed teeth.

"Yes, Corporal." Wiping his sweating hand on his already damp trouser-leg, he got to his feet. "An honour to meet you, Lord Lear."

"And you, Mr Skye." His lordship's hand was cool and smooth, but when Jaime made to pull back he held on, frowning. "What is this?"

"My hand," Jaime said uncertainly.

"Who are you?" Lear demanded, his grip suddenly crushing.

"No one. No one at all."

"He's really not anyone, your lordship," Brigg said, glaring at Jaime from under his woolly brows as though any of this was his fault.

"I don't mean your sort," Lear said to Brigg sharply without looking his way. "He's one of ours."

"I'm not. I'm not anyone." Jaime was now sweating terribly, and succeeded in pulling his slick hand from Lear's fearsome grasp. Lear retreated a step, looking from Jaime to his hand and back.

"I'll need him to come with me," he said to the corporal.

"With all due respect, your lordship," Brigg said, gesturing at the untended desks, "I can hardly spare the man-power."

"Your staffing practices are not my concern, Corporal. This man needs to come with me at once."

Nothing Jaime or the corporal said moved Lear in the slightest. Whatever authority he answered to, it clearly outweighed the patent office, and so it was that Jaime found himself in his coat and hat, leaving his office at half-ten in the morning in the company of the extraordinary man he had vowed to completely ignore.

With his silk hat over his long hair and a black frock coat over his red brocade, Lord Lear was less confronting, though there was no disguising his wealth, not merely by his clothes but by his presumptuous manner. "Now tell me who you really are," he said with a calculating smile as he lead Jaime away from Cathcart House.

"Should we not be speaking somewhere private?"

"I only wished to get you away from Brigg. Who were your parents?"

"Horatio James Skye and Sinead O'Day, but—"

"Where were you born?"

"You'd not know it by name."

"Try me."

"Isle of Angels." A crumb of land, a crag of ancient rock that disappeared on a foggy day. "And if you don't mind, what gives you the right to be asking these questions? Sir?"

"I apologize for not introducing myself more appropriately but I only wish to make so much known to Corporal Brigg. I am Adrian Eustace Rowland, Lord Regent of the House of Lear, Magister of Ellswen and Inheritor of the Western Isles, at your obedient service. As one might expect from my background, I am affiliated with the official body of English craftsmen and -women, and as such I am under certain obligations to make inquiries whenever I encounter someone unknown to the Society. Such as yourself. Where were you schooled?"

"With all due respect, Lord Lear, I'd like first to know why any of this is at all important."

The man frowned, the leaf-green rings of his irises seeming to glow. "If you don't know, then it matters doubly."

"I don't understand. I don't want anything to matter. I just want to be left alone. And what if Brigg sacks me?"

The obnoxious fop laughed in his face. "He won't."

"How can you know what Corporal Brigg will or won't do?"

"You don't have the slightest idea who I am, do you?" Lear said with a frown.

"My apologies for not being not current with the members of the peerage."

"I'm not a peer."

"Then how are you a lord?"

"There's more than one court of which one might be a lord. Here we are." They were standing by the edge of the Round Pond in Kensington Gardens, its broad surface silvered by the thickening haze of clouds. Nearby, some children were sailing toy boats, their nanny dozing on a bench, the eldest boy with his shoes and stockings off from having to retrieve the vessels when they strayed beyond the reach of the others' sticks.

"You've pulled me from work to take me to the park?" Jaime asked, a queasy feeling creeping up from his toes.

"It's an ideal venue," Lear said, gesturing to the water.

"For what?"

"You really don't understand?"

"You've given me nothing to understand. All I know is some lord of some court has removed me from my workplace against my employer's wishes and mine, to interrogate me and show me a public pond." He pointed at the water just as a fish jumped, making a sizeable splash and sending the swans paddling away.

"That's a start," Lear said happily.

"Do you mean your intention was to make me lose my temper?"

"That is often how one discovers one's abilities."

"What abilities? No, actually I don't care what you have to say. I don't have time for this. I have a job. I have a good job I'm going to lose because I'm standing in a park in the middle of the work day talking to another madman!" The wind had risen as if in proportion to Jaime's thoughtless anger, whipping the pond into sharp waves, the children shrieking as their boats capsized, one after the other.

"And you say you don't understand?" Lear was staring at him with a mingled look of horror and delight, as if Jaime were some peculiar object he'd found in a secret place. "Have you never used your craft with purpose?"

"What craft are you talking about? I'm a patent officer. A civil servant. At least I was, until I let you persuade me to desert my post."

"Brigg won't defy me."

"But I will. Good day to you, *Lord* Lear."

"Skye, wait," Lear said, grabbing his arm as he turned, his hand seeming to burn through Jaime's sleeve.

"Don't touch me!" He yanked his arm from Lear's grasp, the gesture startling another water-bird, which burst unseen from the water's surface, sending spray flying. At the same moment, a peal of thunder tore across the blackened sky.

"Mr Skye, please calm yourself," Lear said, staring around them.

"I will not!" All at once it was raining like the clouds had turned inside out, the pond churned to white, Jaime wet to the skin in seconds. "Of all the days...I can't go back to the office like this!"

"Let me help," said Lear. He put his hand on Skye's sleeve, his touch again seeming hot, wisps of what looked like steam rising from between his fingers, the green in his eyes brightening, the pupils widening as Jaime stared. He felt he was falling into an abyss, some infinitely dark place beyond his understanding. With what seemed extraordinary effort, he closed his eyes.

"Please let me go."

Lear lifted his hand, and Jaime ran. Away from the water, away from the impossible man and the lunatic birds. Back to what he'd thought of as sanity until this morning. Thankfully the rain had ceased by the time he reached Cathcart House. He had liked the building from first sight, for it made exactly no impression, was simply another door with brass fixtures and a plaque beside it, in a row of identically nondescript sandstone buildings.

Brigg was on the steps in his hat and coat, a hand out and his eyes cast heavenward. "There you are, Skye. I worried you'd be caught in that. The clouds do seem to follow you about, don't they?"

"I'm very sorry, sir. I didn't expect to be so long."

"Yes, he'll do that to one," Brigg sighed. "At any rate, I'm closing up shop for the day. We've nothing pressing on the roster. You take yourself home and get dry, there's a good chap. Can't have you catching cold when we're running on such limited staff."

"Yes, sir."

"And Lear, did he..."

"I answered his lordship's questions," Jaime replied quickly, for Brigg was a sly interrogator who could sense one's indiscretions from the length of one's hesitation to answer.

"And then what happened?" he pressed.

"I'm afraid I may have overstepped, sir. I lost my temper and said some things I regret."

"Yes, his lordship will do that to just about anyone," Brigg said, nodding sagely. "See you tomorrow."

Though the rain had freshened the city's air, Jaime himself stank of panicky sweat and damp wool. His shoes were soaked, his stockings squishing with each step, even though his mouth was parched. The encounter with Lear had shaken him badly, and he stopped in at the public house at the bottom of his street.

"Same as usual, Mr Skye?"

He nodded and the stooping tavern-keeper poured him a tumbler of still water. He drank it back like a sot drinks his first gin of the day, in a single gulping swallow. "Another."

The man thought him a drunk gone on the dry, as did the serving girl and those regular customers who knew his face. He allowed them to think so, for he had no explanation for the comfort he derived from the act, even though it seemed he could taste every particle of mud, every foot that had ever stepped in the river from which the water was drawn. But it did its magic, quelled his baseless panic, and he drank the second glass more slowly. He paid a penny for the favour of never being expected to buy beer, then carried on to his rooming house, a narrow building at the top end of the winding street.

Mrs Meldrum was a fastidious landlady, keeping the house with the same pride she kept her widowed self. When he came in she was polishing the grand cheval glass in the hall, a pristine apron over her dress of dull grey, its collar of crepe though Mr Meldrum had passed some eighteen years prior.

"Oh Mr Skye, not again?" she said kindly, taking in his wet clothes.

"It looked clear this morning," he replied, the scent of lemon and beeswax fizzing in his nose.

Something startled her and she covered her mouth. "Beg my pardon. I don't mean to laugh at you. I've just realized how funny it is that a man with your name should be so often caught in the rain."

"Yes. Very funny."

"Are you not well, Mr Skye?"

She had a right to ask, for they were on good terms and it was unlike him to be so short with her. "You must excuse me, Mrs Meldrum. I've had a very trying day."

After receiving her consolations, he went up to his room to undress. Not merely his jacket but his shirt was wet, and his trousers from hem to knee. And his hair, and every part of him save one perfectly dry patch on his left sleeve. The place where Lord Lear had touched him. Jaime placed his hand on the same spot, the fabric prickling under his sweating palm.

"Who are you?" he asked the empty room.

He spent the next several weeks in fear of finding out, of seeing that red brocade, hearing that liquid voice. He changed the route he walked to work to avoid passing lilac bushes. At night he was plagued with dreams about falling into black water which swirled around him in inky tendrils like seaweed, like tangled black curls.

If he only had something else with which to occupy his mind. For every kind of reason he was no longer on speaking terms with his foster-family, and his intractable habit of going publicly insane then disappearing into hospital had worn away at his few friendships, leaving him with this narrow life of bureaucratic subservience and lonesome apathy. A long cold night through which Lear had come streaking like a blazing star.

As time passed, Jaime looked over his shoulder less often for that flash of red, no longer leapt from his chair every time Brigg opened his office door. Yet when he smelled that floral pungency in the entry of Cathcart House, he ran. Upstairs, against his expectations, for hadn't he made a pact with himself to refuse any and all offers made by that pompous pseudo-aristocrat? At the door to the patent office he stalled, but the scent of Lear had grown no stronger, and after dabbing his sweating face with his already moist handkerchief Jaime carried on, keeping his eyes down as he scurried to his desk.

The letter sat precisely in the middle of his blotter. It was from this that the soft tickle of scent came, emanating from its thick stock. It bore only his name on the front: Mr J. Skye, and on the back an intricate seal of silvery wax. He left it where it was while he fetched a cup of coffee from the canteen. When he returned, Pickford was in conversation with Brigg in the door to his office, and Jaime slid the letter under his blotter and went about his morning.

Without success, for the smell of that preposterous man's letter was thick in his nose and buzzing in his brain. He was almost glad to see Tyburn, and listened with approximate interest to his retelling of a spree last night involving a game of dice and a woman's glove, which had all gone to causing him such delay this morning.

Tyburn then put up his feet on his desk and went to sleep. Pickford was out on a job, Brigg was in his office being Brigg, and Jaime had no recourse. With his letter opener, he pried off the seal, something about its oily surface uninviting to the touch. The paper was heavy, textured yet smooth, like the feel of stone. Lear's sloping handwriting was that of two hundred years ago, the diphthongs merged, his 's' with a long tail like an 'f,' so that Jaime had to read the letter twice.

Mr Skye,

My humblest salutations. It was put to me that the tenor of our prior interaction merited some action on my part. May I therefore commence with an apology for my overly familiar treatment of you. If you are as you claim unaware of your own nature and the Society into which it permits you, then the fault is wholly mine for any inhospitality which may have marred our first meeting.

If it so please you, I will happily explain your relevance to my interests and the nature of the gifts of which you are so unfortunately ignorant. Having familiarized myself with the details of your mishandling by Ordinary medical philosophies, again I claim wholly the fault for mis-

representing my orientation to said philosophies. I have for the purpose engaged a private room at the Magisters' Club, of which I am a member in excellent standing, and welcome you to join me for a convivial luncheon, accompanied by a surfeit of explanation.

Yours in light,

A. Lear

It concluded with a jumble of made-up titles and the location of his club. His head feeling pressed in a vice, Jaime read the letter through a third time. He had never heard of Lear's club, not that he paid much attention to the establishments of the upper crust. He didn't even recognize the name of the street, which probably meant it was tucked away in some tony suburb where even the footmen were better dressed than Jaime could ever hope to achieve on his wage. It was none the less a chance to set Lear straight and hopefully make clear that what Jaime most wanted from him was to be permanently left alone.

THE MAGISTERS' CLUB

T he Magisters' club was a soot-blackened Georgian house on the corner of Half-Moon Passage, a wigging slip of brick lane that lead back to Alie Street and which smelled of the effluent from the public house at the other end. Standing before it, Jaime assured himself of Lear's invitation in his pocket, unsure what scrutiny he was about to undergo.

He glanced up and down the narrow lane to be sure he was alone, then swiped his handkerchief over his short hair to dry his sweating scalp, bit away a straggling thread from the frayed cuff of his jacket. Nothing to be done about its sagging shoulders or generally poor fit or the fact that between his wretched clothes and cropped hair and sallow skin and sour odour he resembled nothing so much as a convalescent the first day out of the sickroom.

The tall black door of the club bore no handle, only a tarnished brass knocker in the form of a scaled creature with a fish's body and a gargoyle's face. The cast was so realistic Jaime half feared it would squirm when he grasped it, the sound heavy, as if it rang from the cellar.

The door opened of its own accord. Then it cleared its throat. Or rather, the diminutive man who had opened it did so. Barely over four feet tall, with a narrow face and eyes of a striking silvery blue that showed hardly any pupil, he was crisply dressed in a newly styled tailcoat, his expression precisely what Jaime expected of the door manager of a gentlemen's club: perfectly blank, save for the slightest tilt of his eyebrows to suggest Jaime had better get on with explaining himself.

"Mr Skye. Welcome," the slight man said without a hint of question or derision before Jaime could gather his wits. He stepped aside for Jaime to enter. "My name is Kristoff, and you may consider me at your service. I might begin by taking your overcoat."

As Jaime slipped off his mackintosh an ordinarily sized young man stepped out of an open doorway to take it from him. He opened a heavily carved door behind Jaime which turned out to lead to a capacious cloak room. The gunpowder scent of Lear was everywhere, and Jaime pinched the tip of his nose to keep from sneezing as he followed Kristoff up the grand staircase dominating the left of the entry hall.

Everything was heavy and luxurious, the staircase a grandiose enterprise of carven oak, the mossy carpet swallowing their footsteps. The panelled walls were intricately painted with scenes of exotic locales--cities with minarets, verdant green valleys, windswept mountain peaks--the glossy colours so vivid one might swear the pictures lived. Otherwise the club was similar to the few stately homes he'd been in, with high ceilings and cool air and an atmosphere of imperturbable privilege that made his stomach knot about itself.

Two people were in conversation on the landing at the top of the broad stairs: a fair, pink-cheeked man with very pale hair and a similar style of dressing to Lear, with silver buckles on his pointed shoes and a cerulean frock coat heavily embroidered with a pattern of vines and bold mauve flowers. His ebony-skinned companion was no less flamboyant though in quite another manner, wearing a floor-skimming robe of a striking geometric print in red and yellow, his bare toes protruding from leather sandals. They were speaking in animated French, the white man seeming to plead some case, the African maintaining steadfast refusal.

"Non, et non, et non, Hercule. Pas possible," he said with a chopping motion of his hand.

"We'll see," the white man said with a rueful twist of his broad mouth. He glanced at Jaime then looked again. "Kristoff, have we a new member?" he asked with a dazzling smile.

"A guest, your lordship," Kristoff replied, his voice too deep for his slight build.

"A guest of whom?"

"Of another member, your lordship. Do excuse us."

One lunatic semi lord was enough for Jaime's fragile senses, and he kept his eyes lowered as they passed the men, his nose itching like he'd shoved peppercorns up it, the scent like burnt sugar. This of course meant looking at the floor which on this level was tiled in squares of black and white marble. Which then began to tilt precipitously so that the broad hall became a valley... a valley that Kristoff walked smoothly across, because it was an illusion caused by the clever laying of differently sized tiles. A trick of the eye so persuasive that Jaime hesitated before following, his feet not wholly convinced there would be a floor to meet them.

Rather than being painted, the walls here were hung with portraits of well-dressed men and occasionally women of centuries passed, posing among allegorical goods as was the fashion in other times: a skull for mortality, an apple for love, a cage of birds for either freedom or confinement, he couldn't recall which. The paintings included stranger objects as well, mechanical devices and glass phials of brightly coloured liquids. The gunpowder scent had become part of the general miasma of sense impressions crowding Jaime's mind, and he gasped at the first breath of lilac, which grew stronger as they approached a closed door.

Kristoff held up a hand, the palm facing the door. There was a click and the door swung inward. He entered and stood aside, bowing slightly to the occupant. "Your lordship, Mr Skye to see you."

"Thank you, Kristoff. I'll call for the meal shortly."

He'd forgotten the sound of Lear's voice, the bell-like resonance, the country accent with the Oxford inflection, as if East Anglia had maintained own court and king. Dressed in dark green, his overlong hair bound into a queue, Lear rose from the table, shook Jaime's hand briefly, invited him to take the other chair. The room was less grandiose than the house, the walls papered prettily with vines and flowers, the flames in the tiled hearth tinged with emerald. With his white cravat and elaborately embroidered waistcoat, his buckskin breeches worn to whiteness, Lear resembled a Defoe hero, and looked wholly native to his strangely lovely environs, leaving Jaime to feel like a dirty handbill pasted on the side of a cathedral: shabby and worn, inconsequential as a flea.

"Thank you for coming, Mr Skye," Lear said as he resumed his seat.

"Oh. Yes. Thank you for the invitation."

"Please do allow me to once again apologise for my confrontational approach the other day. It's rare that I meet an Ordinary who turns out not to be."

"I am, though. I am very ordinary. Believe me." *Please, believe me.*

Lear shifted in his chair, a subtle smile tugging at his lips. "Mr Skye, you are not Ordinary."

"Whether I am or not, I'm not at all interesting."

Lear frowned, though the smile lingered. "May I make an extrapolation, Mr Skye?"

"If it pleases you."

"From our first meeting and what I've discovered since, I believe your upbringing has entailed a number of extremely unpleasant experiences. All of which may have been visited upon you without your knowledge of their likely outcomes, or indeed of the causes which so motivated your guardians to treat you as they did."

Jaime was well used to parsing medical verbiage about his own ailments. "What do you know about my...upbringing?"

"You are, for better or worse, a matter of public record, Mr Skye."

"I know that. I've had enough doctors remand me for institutional care." And a magistrate demand it on pain of a far worse form of confinement.

"They were wrong to do so." Lear was frowning, the leaping flames reflecting in his dark eyes, and Jaime felt for the first time the power in the man.

"I was a danger to myself and others," he explained, as he did to everyone eventually. "It was the best decision for everyone."

"It was a lie," Lear said sharply.

"How can you know that? With all due respect, your lordship."

"Never mind titles. I'm happy for you to address me as Adrian. And I know because I know what you are, Mr Skye." Grinning, he sat back, his eyes running over Jaime, a gaze too familiar. Doubly cursed, every part of him at odds with normal life, the other man's presence confirming him as the source of all Jaime's recent anguish, all those dreams of swirling curls and honeyed words from which he woke damp and gasping.

"I don't know what you're talking about."

"Perhaps because you've never had it explained to you."

"I know well enough my own nature, your lordship. My personal conduct is no one's business but mine. And may I say how inappropriate I feel it is for you to be interrogating my past without my knowledge. Tell me what you want of me, or I shan't tolerate your intrusions any longer."

He waited for the tirade, for the operation of privilege, for dismissal, but Lear was still smiling as he replied. "Mr Skye, at Kensington you caused water to spout from the pond."

"I did no such thing."

"You drew a storm from a clear sky and threw it at me."

Jaime shook his head, less in denial than sheer disbelief. "I don't know what you mean. I didn't do a thing."

"You are a water-worker Mr Skye. It obeys your will, whether you intend it or not. Look, I can do it too." Lear set his hand on the table, palm up. In the middle of his palm lay a drop of water. The drop swelled, growing to fill his cupped hand until water began spilling onto the tablecloth. It might have been running blood for the churning horror in Jaime's guts.

"Please stop. Whatever tricks you're playing with my mind, whatever illusion, stop it at once."

"This is no illusion, Mr Skye." Lear had taken a glass and let it fill with the water running from his empty hand. He now placed it before Jaime, who sprang up from the table as if he'd been offered poison, making the water slosh in the glass.

"For the love of God, stop this torture!" Ashamed, enraged, he hid his face. He was sweating obscenely, his hands dripping with it, his head swimming from the hot fire, which had begun sputtering weirdly, as if the wood was wet. Lear was a demon, a villain, rooting out Jaime's deepest frailties then hurling them in his face. He hadn't gone a step towards the door when Lear caught hold of his arm.

"Let me go!"

"I want only to help you."

"Then you can..."

Jaime meant to say stop. But why would he ever want this to stop, this flood of golden light pouring over him? Or was it welling up from within, spilling from his every cell, until he was nothing but the light...

It softly ebbed, quieter and quieter still, until it became a single glowing mote, a star above the ocean. "What happened?" he asked as the room resolved around him.

"I might explain in future," Lear said quietly. "But it won't mean anything to you yet."

"Why is it stopping?"

"Because it must. Please, sit down."

He did not particularly want to, but Lear knew best, for at his first step his legs nearly buckled under him. He sunk gratefully into the plush armchair by the hearth where the emerald-edged flames once more crackled merrily. The carven arms of the chair resembled a lion's paws, and he curled his fingers comfortably over the burnished wood. Lear was busy at the table so Jaime sat and watched the fire and petted the wooden paws and managed to think of nothing else for a number of very pleasant minutes. When had he last been so continually content? Even that dire consideration wasn't enough to spoil his sense of safety.

Lear had taken off his fitted jacket, the loose sleeves of his linen shirt furthering the illusion that he might turn pirate given adequate provocation. He offered Jaime a full glass of clear liquid with ice floating in it. "Gin and water. Entirely ordinary."

"Have you just water? I don't take alcohol."

"Certainly."

He poured a tall glass which Jaime downed in one pull. With a curious expression Lear poured him another, which suffered a similar swift fate. "I didn't expect you needed to drink at all," Lear said as Jaime wiped his mouth.

"It helps, after. When I've had a bad turn. I don't know what you did, but thank you."

"I very much owed you, Mr Skye."

"Jaime. Please."

"I must once more apologise, Jaime. I have presumed much."

"I would have thought you knew you had a madman on your hands."

"You're not mad, Jaime."

Words he'd heard before. "Yes, one mustn't call it that anymore. I'm suffering from a mental aberration. Or a neurotic episode. Or exhaustion. Or—"

"There is nothing whatsoever wrong with your mind, Jaime."

"There must be."

"No. You've been deceived. By those who knew no better."

"I wasn't safe on my own."

"That's no reason for you to have been incarcerated."

"I wasn't in prison. I was in hospital." Even though the doors were always locked and he was at times strapped to his bed. There'd been no other way to keep him alive.

"I don't know who it is you're trying to protect," Lear said with an edge of irritation.

"Me. I'm protecting myself." He owed no further explanation. Not to a man who had taken the liberty of uncovering his history and was now obliging him to dissect it. The bright star of hope was dimming, lost in the same old fog of despair.

Lear reclined in his soft chair, untouched by such agonies, gazing at Jaime with the open face of privilege. "Did you know your grandmother?" he asked without preface. "Your father's mother, that is."

"Why does that matter?"

"You're the son of a Skye. In my world, that means a great deal. Particularly if you've been denied knowledge of your heritage. Why did your parents teach you nothing?"

All his inquiries and this was unknown to him? "They never had a chance. They died, my lord. I was raised in fosterage."

Lear's puzzled look turned to alarm. "Died?" he repeated, a catch in his fluid voice.

"I've been told it's not uncommon."

"How?"

"I'm shocked you don't know, given your interest in my past."

"Not all information was so easily obtained," he murmured.

"Then allow me to enlighten your lordship. Horatio and Sinead Skye were arrested for sedition. They were extradited, to be tried in England. The ship sank with all hands."

"You can't mean they drowned."

"Is there another term for it?"

"Horatio Skye could not have drowned," he said with precision. "Why weren't you sent to Mammy Skye? Your grandmother? By Jove, who let this happen?"

"I was a child. What could I have done?"

"I don't mean you. Indeed, not a bit of this is your fault."

"So they've told me. That it's a disease."

"No!" Lear said with vehemence. "You are not sick. You are not mad. You are...you are simply not Ordinary, Mr Skye."

"Madmen usually aren't."

Lear spat a strange word, the flames seeming to flare in reply. He glanced sharply at the fire but it carried on with its cheery flicker. Perhaps Lear was the madman. Or they were both mad, in which case this meeting was beyond futile, was Jaime flirting with disaster, inviting a relapse, another disappearance.

"I'm sorry but I cannot stay. I wish you'd not contact me again, Lord Lear. I don't know what purpose you intend for me but I want no part of it. I just want to be left alone." Politeness and privilege could go and whistle, and he lurched from his chair and started for the door.

"No!" Lear shouted as if in fear and sprang up after him. "Please, Jaime, don't leave."

Presumptuous as ever, he grabbed for Jaime, who snarled as he wrenched his arm from Lear's grasp. "I told you, don't touch me!"

The room was suddenly cast into darkness, the fire doused as if by a bucket, acrid smoke billowing from the matted ash. Somewhere a glass shattered, then Lear said another foreign word. A glow appeared, emanating from a bright point on Lear's chest, spreading as the smoke around it cleared.

He was gathering the clouds with his hands, herding them like reeking sheep towards the hearth where they subsided into the coals, leaving behind clear air and the scent of burnt lilac. The light from his brooch dimmed as Lear bent over the hearth. Jaime stayed where he was, his back against the door, his hands numb, his heart as well. This was how it always went, the start of his every decline, with his reckless temper and another's fear, and the very best thing for him to do was leave and never come back. Never see Lear again. Quit the patent office, move north or south or anywhere, change his name like he'd always intended and forget he'd ever been Jaime Skye.

"Is...is she alive?" he found himself asking.

"Your grandmother?" Lear said, getting to his feet. "Yes."

"That thing," he stammered, for he had begun trembling, from fear and from the chill of wet cloth against his skin. "Please...what you did before..."

"It won't be as effective, but I will try." Lear wiped his fingers clean of ashes on a cloth from the table, then came to Jaime and gently placed his right hand on the top of Jaime's head. Again came the golden light, but so very slowly, a treacly drip rather than a deluge, so sweet that when it reached his heart he began to cry. Softly, a trail of tears, as salt as the sea.

"Adrian...who am I?"

Lear lifted his hand and the golden light receded, seeming to gather back into the gleaming brooch on his left lapel, which stayed alit, a star in the darkness. "You are James Skye," he said, as though to speak the name was an honour. "Inheritor of the Northwest, Defender of Angels."

Jaime wanted to laugh, deny he had any significance to the world, even as the words raised the hairs on the back of his neck. "Go on, then. What else have you got?"

Adrian smiled, the creases round his eyes putting to Jaime the question of how old the man truly was. "As you like. You possess a highly prized and exceedingly rare facility for manipulating an element of the manifested world. I would like to be able to tell you how exactly this facility functions, where it was first recorded and so on, but to be blunt and much to my embarrassment we simply don't know. So many water-workers have lost their lives and had their work destroyed by pogroms and witch burnings and such that the lineage has been scattered. The talent is however latent in certain families, such as yours."

"I was told it's madness that runs in the Skyes."

"No, Jaime," he said with a sad shake of his head. "It's the cruelty of the Ordinary who misunderstand your gift that has caused you to believe yourself unwell."

At this he had to laugh "Gift? It's a damned curse. It's ruined my life."

"If you'd grown up among those who understood—"

"Well, I didn't. And this is the result." He plucked at his sodden shirt front, his drenched hair, gestured to the doused fire, the fallen pitcher of water. "Heaven help me, I can't even manage to..." What was the good in concealing anything? Lear would have it out of him eventually, face to face or through his ferreting. "I tried to take my life. Did you not read about that in the doctors' notes?" he asked as Adrian startled. "The fool I am, I tried to drown myself. I tried and I couldn't. I was under for an hour. Spat up water afterwards for days."

Lit only by the up-pointing glow from his strange brooch, Adrian's face was a carven mask of agony. "It means little, but I'm so very sorry you've had to live this way. But that can change."

"You can't change what's passed."

"Yes. But I can help you have a better future."

"Cure me."

"You're not ill," he said gently, his smile hitching at Jaime's next words.

"But could you stop it? Whatever it is I do, can you make it not ever happen again? I don't want to live like this."

"Jaime, I know this is a shock to you, but your family are—"

"My family are dead."

"Not your grandmother. Not you."

"There'll be no more Skyes after me if I have the say of it."

At this Lear stepped back sharply, his expression severe. "Even were I to agree, it is an impossible risk. You should expect to die."

"I should be so lucky." His throat was raw, and without Lear blocking his way he stumbled to the table, but it was the pitcher of water which had broken during his outburst, drenching the table. Because of his outburst, because of him, because of the monster inside him: unnamed, untamed, a danger to himself and the world.

"Jaime, please," Lear said gently, coming near but not touching him as he stood at the unlit table searching among the glasses for any still holding a drop. "I can teach you to master your talent. Make use of it rather than letting it overwhelm you. Show you that, despite what the Ordinary world believes, there's nothing at all wrong with you."

"Doctors aplenty have said there was."

"After all they've done...do you still trust them?"

ON HAMPSTEAD HEATH

And so it was that Jaime stumbled out of bed the next morning at first light to trudge up to Hampstead Heath ponds to try moving water with his mind. Last night after their surprisingly basic meal of roast fowl, Lear had kindly dried the moisture from Jaime's clothes by laying his hand on Jaime's sleeve and thinking it away, a trick he had assured Jaime he would be able to learn for himself.

Not even Mrs Meldrum was awake as Jaime crept down the unlit stairs, his boots in hand. He sat on the bottom stair to lace them then slipped outside. As he came around the bend he stopped. A gleaming carriage with an intricate coat of arms on the door stood at the end of the crooked mews, swathed in fog. As Jaime approached, the driver descended and opened the door.

"Mr Skye, I'm to assist you." Despite the wool scarf wrapping the man's head to his ears, his voice was perfectly clear, like he had spoken the words directly into Jaime's ear.

"You work for Lord Lear?"

After a hesitation which suggested this was not at all the case, the man inclined his head. "Yes, Mr Skye. Will you come?"

His unimpeded voice seemed to draw no echo from the close of buildings. His eyes...weren't there, his head a featureless shape, an impenetrable blankness between the top of the scarf and the brim of his silk hat.

"I may be unusually durable but I do still feel the cold, Jaime," said a familiar, human voice from inside the carriage. "Please do get in."

After assuring himself that there was a completely present pair of horses attached to the front of the vehicle, Jaime climbed into the warm cab, taking the bench opposite Lear. Though evidently old the carriage was pure luxury, with velvet drapes and padded seats and a comforting aroma of oiled wood and warm pastry.

"Thank you for this," Jaime said as the carriage rocked into motion. "Though I don't recall telling you where I lived."

"Presumptuousness is one of my more consistent habits, I admit." Even for a tramp through a meadow, Lear was dressed to perfection in an old fashioned riding habit of crimson wool, a snowy white stock delineating his sharp jaw. "Bearing that in mind, I shall now inform you of the society to which you most evidently belong."

The Royal Society of Magisters: an elite of the strangely empowered and obscurely educated, all bound by a self-made constitution that adhered generally to British Law while sounding as if it stood apart and very slightly above. Magisters—craftspeople in casual parlance, for the talents appeared across all economic classes—based their craft on the lore of an arcane web of ancient alchemists and Gnostics and holy orders of knights, many of whom had become victims of Inquisitorial prejudice, the lines of succession further eroded by successive genera- tions of rational governance. The Society seemed to have had great sway during the Napoleonic Wars with commensurate loss of life, such that they had held a neutral position on conflicts since, certain individuals' efforts notwithstanding.

By the time Lear got to describing the role of the Skye family, it had begun to feel like one of Brigg's longer lectures on artillery pieces and the innumerable ways in which they might explode. Jaime nodded and blinked and performed other proofs of an understanding he did not possess, numbed not only by the overabundance of new information but by the early morning, the sway of the carriage, the brilliant presence of Lear, glowing like a ripe apple in autumn sunshine, smelling like hot flowers and rust.

At last the faceless driver stopped to let them out by the viaduct bridge, a little to the east of the Vale of Heath. Leaving the carriage by the roadside, they descended through a band of trees to the pond below. The mist was denser here, the air cold and thick with the smell of rotting vegetation and the stones of the bridge, which was nearly invisible across the still water.

"Do you like pork pies?" Lear asked, as if that was at all relevant.

"Er, yes. Generally."

"Good. Eat one." He had already taken a cloth-wrapped pastry from the pannier on his hip and was offering it to Jaime. "You'll want something in you for this work."

Though they'd been in the carriage for over an hour, the pie was steaming, like he'd bought it minutes ago, the meat inside of shocking tenderness. As well Lear produced hot tea in a pair of handle-less cups, though Jaime wasn't sure from where. They sat on a fallen tree and ate and drank without talking as the mist began to brighten towards the east.

"Now, Mr Skye—" Lear began, setting his cup beside the pannier on the grass by his feet.

"Jaime. If you please."

"Of course, Jaime. As you know, your affinity with water gives you a great deal of sway with the weather. You've seen how the clouds reply to your emotions. They should as well respond to your more direct intentions. Bearing that in mind, I'd like you to try lifting this fog."

"How should I do it?"

"It may be as simple as thinking, away from me."

"It may be? You mean you don't know?"

"I've never met someone as talented as you are, yet who didn't know they were. I'm not certain how one starts from scratch." He stood up and brushed the pastry crumbs from his hands. A single crumb had adhered to his chin, engendering in Jaime a near unbearable need to brush it away as he joined Lear at the pond's edge.

It was one of the smaller bodies of water on the heath, surrounded by a guard of trees save for where the bridge crossed at the narrower end. "Can you perhaps tell me how you'd do it?" Jaime asked, for he hadn't a notion how even to start.

Lear frowned briefly. "I can't say for certain that your talent functions in the same way as mine."

"As far as I know, I haven't any such talent at all, so it might help if you gave me something to go on."

"Very well. Mist is merely water vapour suspended in the lower atmosphere, yes?"

"If you say so."

Lear regarded him curiously before returning his attention to the pond. "I swear by all the gods," he said under his breath, "whosoever's choice it was to send you into Ordinary fosterage, they can expect to answer to me. These are things you should know like your own name. But as you said," he went on brightly, "we can't change what's passed. I can only hope to illuminate your future." He rubbed his hands together then shook them as if shaking off rain.

"Should I be doing that?" Jaime asked.

"If you like. Now, were it to me, I should think my way down to the infinitesimal scale, then attempt to interfere with the protean particles' direction of flow."

"Would you now?"

"That means precisely nothing to you, I know."

"I'll try it like you said before, how about?"

"But don't merely think it, see it. Imagine it working."

In his imagination was like to be the only way of it working at all, but Jaime set aside his meagre expectations and thought about the mist not being there. And maybe it stirred in response, but the sun was rising behind them and drying the air and after perhaps ten minutes Adrian asked him to stop.

He stood musing, tapping his folded knuckle against his chin. "Right. Let's try something more obvious." He pointed at the unruffled surface of the pond.

"I can't dry up all that."

"Why would you want to do so? No, I only want to see if you can affect it. Cause a flow, a ripple."

"I don't know how."

"Yes, but you've done similar without intending it."

"Would it not be easier to just throw a rock?" he asked tartly.

"Yes, but don't. Simply imagine it. Imagine you are throwing a pebble," Lear said, his voice taking on a soothing cadence. "Make a throwing motion if you like. Feel the stone leave your hand. See it in your mind's eye, arcing from your hand into the water. Hear it strike, see the ripples. Can you imagine all these things together?"

"I think so."

"Good. Now try it."

And he did, thought of everything that happened in the act of pitching a small stone into water as he stared at a single spot on the pond's surface, willing it with something like sincerity to move. Anything. A drop, a wobble, a ripple. Nothing at all, and he released the breath he'd been holding. Like an insult, a fish chose that moment to flick the surface with its tail.

"Of all the cheek, for that fish to pop up just then."

"Try it again. But this time don't hold your breath."

He returned his attention to the silvery water, but the early sunshine was giving way to slatey clouds, the wind plucking at the water so his own effects if any went undetected.

"There," he said as a raindrop struck the surface. "No wonder it looked like it was working."

"It is working perfectly well," Lear said. "Though it's evident you don't feel you're succeeding." He gestured to the clouds, which had quite filled this region of the sky.

"It's only a little rain. It's nothing to do with me."

"It has everything to do with you."

"What is it you even want from me?"

Lear's sunny smile fell, though his eyes still shone. "I want only to help you, Jaime."

"Yes, but what's in it for you?"

"Must everything be done for one's own advantage?" Lear asked with a laugh. Jaime said nothing, the question of a sort that Brigg might use to lead a fool to a confession. "Very well. Let us say I'm hoping to exorcise certain...curiosities." That smile again, and a telling glance, a challenge and invitation in one.

"So that's it," Jaime said as he stepped back from the edge of the pond and from Lear's bewitching presence. "That's why you've brought me all the way out here."

"I thought it best we not be seen. Have I done something wrong?"

"If not, it's only as I'll not be giving you the chance."

The wind had lifted, thrashing at the trees, and as a peal of thunder split the air Jaime made a dash past Lear to the path leading up to the roadway. Somehow the shit outpaced him, stepping from the trees to bar his way.

"Jaime, please tell me what's wrong. I don't understand why you're angry."

"Don't bother to lie. Not now that I've found you out."

"Jaime, you must explain."

"What's there to explain? You're the one who's dragging desperate men off to the woods. You and your masked man. The worst is," he spat before Lear could interject, "you're not even the first who's done this to me. What a fool I am!"

No more than a stone's throw away, a searing bolt of pure incandescence struck the water, the air sizzling as a cannonade of thunder broke directly above. Lear turned to him, aghast. "You are doubtless a fool if you deny the evidence of your senses."

"I have no senses, remember? Madman?" And he slapped his own forehead. "For all I know this is a dream. A fever. Hallucinations."

"Jaime, you know that's not true." Lear made a grab for his arm, the presumptuous arse, but Jaime leapt back.

"Don't you dare!" Another bolt of lightning struck, igniting the air and nearly blinding him.

"Turn the storm, Jaime!" Lear shouted into the wind. "You're going to get us killed!"

"I'm not doing anyth—" The first two times, it had felt like molten joy. Today the golden light was a firestorm that immolated his rage in a single breath and left him scorched to the bone. He fell, or just about, Lear's fearsome grip on his upper arm nailing him upright. "Make it stop…"

The brilliance faded, the wood and the water coming back into view. Lear aided him back down the path where they sat together on the fallen tree. Neither spoke, and though the rain had begun in earnest Jaime hardly felt it.

"That was perhaps overmuch," Lear said at length.

"If I ask for your help it's one thing, but you can't go about...illuminating people without warning."

"I apologise. I will ask you in future. Though to be fair I did so to preserve our lives."

Jaime sat up cautiously. Aside from his inevitably damp shirt, he was dry, as if the rain which peppered the surface of the pond had left him untouched. He dared to glance up. There was the rain, a most unusual sight from below, the drops winking out of existence as they struck a vague shining in the air some six inches above their heads. "How is it you can do that, anyway? The golden light, I mean."

"Manipulation."

"Of what, though?"

"What do you know of the brain?"

"More than most lay-folk, I expect. Once the doctors started talking about drilling holes in my head, I said to myself I ought to know what was in there."

"They didn't trepan you, did they?" Lear asked, his eyes flying open in horror.

"No. No, I refused. That was a battle but they relented. Mainly as no one offered to pay. Which was curious as my donor hadn't shied from the other bills."

"Your donor?"

"No one wants a strange boy as their foster, see? I got passed around like a bad penny, house to house, whenever I got to be too much for them."

"Were you argumentative?"

"Just strange. But really properly strange. Changeling, the other children would call me, right before I got sent on to another house. My first long stay in hospital, I came out to find there was no one at all. Except someone had left a packet of money with the head of hospital. I can't believe he gave it me. A hundred pounds it was. I'd have starved otherwise."

"How old were you when this happened?"

"Twelve."

"By the gods..." Lear whispered, deathly pale. "And you've been on your own ever since?"

"So to speak. I've not had to pay a doctor ever, but I've not ever learned who's supporting me."

"Supports you but never chose to adopt you?"

"At least it's something. I'd be dead otherwise, no lie." He touched his neck, where the rain had at last broken through. Lear glanced up and the viscous presence in the air seemed to thicken, the rain once more evaporating before it could reach them.

"You've been robbed, Jaime," Lear said, and the hitch of sadness in his melodious voice was a tiny heartbreak all its own.

"A few times, actually."

"I don't mean of money. I mean of your life."

"Oh, that. That doesn't matter."

"It does," he said sternly. "I for one would have never let you suffer so if I'd only known."

"What could you have done?"

"For someone of your talent, your centrality to the Society's founding principles and motivations, to be subjected to the prejudices of the Ordinary is tantamount to criminal. I should have brought you up myself if only I'd known."

"How? We're not so different in age."

"We are, though." Lear grimaced. "Though I don't expect you'll believe me."

"That's for sure. Pardon me if I'm wrong but you can't be more than forty, can you? You'd have to use bootblack to keep that hair of yours from showing grey."

"I don't age as others do." The grimace was now a smirk. "Partly ancestry, partly vanity, but I am very much older than I look."

"How old? Fifty?" Lear shook his glossy head. "Sixty?" He only smiled, and yes there were creases by his eyes but his throat was sleek and his cheeks smooth and if Jaime guessed any further he'd gravely insult the man. "Please just tell me, will you?"

"Very well. I am one hundred and twenty seven years old."

"If you say so."

He laughed, showing a full mouth of very clean teeth. "I didn't expect you to believe me."

"Sorry, but. And for shouting at you. And nearly getting us burnt up."

"And I apologise for my presumptuous stimulation of your nervous system. Shall we have more tea?"

"If there's any to be had."

Lear made a sort of trilling whistle through his nice teeth and his groomsman stepped from behind a nearby tree. "Fetch the tea things, will you, Voight?"

The faceless man inclined his blank of a head, turned on his heel and was gone, simply gone. A moment later, the sound of the carriage door being opened carried across the water.

"What is...who is..."

"Mr Nihilo?" Lear asked, peering into the pannier from where now emerged the scent of stewed fruit and fresh scones. "He's in league with my house, Ellswen."

"Then he is your servant."

"No," Adrian said with a smile. "Mr Nihilo is no one's servant."

"I don't understand."

"You'd be surprised how often I hear people say that."

"Actually, I don't expect I would."

TEA ON THE LAWN

Rather than waiting for Nihilo to return, Lear led them away from the pond, beyond the trees and onto the thick turf of the heath. Nihilo was there, waiting by a blue plaid blanket he had laid on the grass and furnished with an entire tea service: a piping pot, matched cream and sugar, translucent slices of lemon in a small bowl. There was nowhere to sit but on the blanket, which Lear did with a graceful folding of his fine legs and Jaime did with much less elegance. Sitting on his knees on the prickly blanket, he accepted a cup and saucer, gold-rimmed and decorated inside and out with brightly coloured birds.

"Showing off, are we?" Adrian asked as Nihilo transferred a lump of sugar with a pair of ruby-tipped tongs.

"Should one not use the good china for guests?" came the echoless reply.

"I'll not be asking you for a luncheon, I haven't the patience to envelop a marquee."

The man-of-the-house laughed. Or so Jaime presumed, as that voice-that-wasn't produced a low, good humoured pulsing of the air in his vicinity. He departed once they were settled. The foul weather had passed, the brief rain not enough to soak the grass, merely to make it sparkle in the sun. The pond as well, glittering between the trees some hundred yards away. Lear set his cup aside and stretched out his legs, reclining on his elbows. "Is it offensive if I rest for a little while?"

"You're going to sleep here? Out in the open?"

"I've enveloped us in a very reliable force of non-attention. And Voight's around if anyone remains curious."

"Is he enough protection?" Jaime asked, looking around for the suited form.

"I assure you, Mr Nihilo is more than capable of diverting nearly anyone or anything that might consider us interesting." He was already lying down, his arm over his face.

Jaime sat where he was for some time, until his feet had gone numb and Lear's slow breathing suggested he was in fact asleep. Being even less inclined to walk home from the heath than he'd been to walk to it, he settled more comfortably on the blanket. After a little he laid back, resting his head on his crooked arm. Lear was very much asleep, lying on his side, his impossibly young face relaxed, lips a little parted. His lashes were as dark as his hair and too full for a man's. He was, Jaime had to admit, very handsome.

He rolled to his back before Lear stirred and caught him looking. There would go any neutrality, any chance of avoiding the unpleasantly inevitable moment when a man he was coming to trust as his friend became his tormentor. Perhaps true friendship was the lie.

A cloud was bearing towards them, a flat-bottomed hummock of snowy white. The sort that warned of impending rain, though the sky was otherwise an enduring shade of blue. "Go away," he said. "I've been rained on enough." The wind had freshened, and as he watched, the vast hill of cloud began to shear apart. By the time it passed overhead it was a mere wisp, barely dimming the sun. The early rising and difficult morning had sapped his strength and Jaime closed his eyes.

He woke alone. Blinking past the dazzle of midmorning sun, he spied a red coat moving among the trees round the pond. Nihilo was still absent, and Jaime took his time getting to his feet. Lear had paused amid a cluster of aspen and was gazing up into the branches, whistling in startling imitation of a blackcap, which answered back. As a child Jaime had taken many a knock from older boys for trying to stop them from throwing stones at birds or taking their nests, and he left them to what one could argue was a conversation.

His favourite foster homes had been in the countryside, not because the families had been any less suspicious of him but for the pleasure of the environs, the copses and meadows where a child might disappear for delightful hours, free of the interference of either grown-ups or other children. Gleaming prettily, the pond beckoned, and he sat on the edge which here had been fortified with brick, sun-warmed and crumbling at the corners. Unlike the first two touches which had enlivened but not alarmed him, Lear's last laying of hands had broken through some inner barricade, leaving Jaime unguarded, his wounds disclosed. Yet he hadn't fought his way back to sanity only to hide from the world. He had never been mad…

By the time Adrian joined him he had produced a very pretty little show. Droplets leapt from the pond's shuddering surface and fell into their own ripples, spouts of water arcing gracefully around them. "I used to call it 'plip', he said as Adrian crouched beside him. "My secret game. For a time."

"How do you play it?"

"I don't know. Truly, I don't. When I want it to jump, it does."

"How does it make you feel?"

"It doesn't. That is, I don't feel it moving."

"Hmm."

He let the water calm, until once again only the faint current tugged at the surface. "Your guardians kept you from playing such games, didn't they?" Adrian said kindly.

"I took it hard, yes. Until I learned better."

"I'm so sorry, Jaime."

"There were so many times I hoped to die. From the cures, that is. So they'd leave off trying." Trying to cure him of being himself. He had never been mad.

"You needn't tell me anything," Adrian said as Jaime gasped for breath. "I know what they've done to you. And I'm never going to let it happen again."

A fancy, the idle thought of a privileged man. A gift of kindness surpassing even that of his unknown sponsor, who had paid for his cures yet never his livelihood. Paid doctors to disbelieve him, again and again and again. He hunched forward, tears raining from his eyes into the rippling pond, his stomach clenching like he'd swallowed the ocean and it wanted to be let out.

"Jaime," Adrian said, bending near but not touching him. "Jaime, let me take you home."

Home. Safe. Hidden and warm and dry, and he forced himself to nod.

"May I touch you? Softly, I promise." He nodded again, and Adrian laid his hand gently over the back of Jaime's head. The golden wave rose, subsided, bearing away to its healing depths his fear, his pain, his wretched memories, leaving only peace, a beatific sea on which his soul might contentedly drift for all eternity.

"Adrian?"

"Yes?"

"I'm too happy to go home."

"I meant my home."

"Oh. Yes. Because mine is dreadful."

"You deserve so much more."

The carriage was waiting, and though bitter experience had taught him the danger of letting a man take him home, he allowed Lear to help him aboard. Again they sat opposite, though in the close quarters the scent of what must be Lear's magic was giddying.

Magic. Not madness but a kind of magic, though Lear hadn't used the word once. Jaime thought of the water welling up in Lear's hand, last night at the Magisters' club. And the golden light, and Lear drawing the dampness from Jaime's clothes with only a touch and a focused stare. For now the man was quiet, his eyes closed, hands cupped in his lap like a carven monk. Perhaps he felt Jaime's gaze, as he opened his eyes. "Are you feeling better?" he asked kindly.

"Much. In fact, I ought really to be at work."

"I shall write to Brigg and explain your absence."

"How is it that he has to take your orders?"

"It's quite complicated."

"There's not a thing about you that isn't."

Lear laughed, bowing his head. "I accept the charges. If it please you to know, as the bureaucracy of governance has expanded over the centuries, the Magisters' influence has moved from the centre to the margins, as it were."

"There's no more Royal Alchemist?" Jaime said in jest, but Lear replied earnestly.

"Oh no, there's still one of those. But he no longer has a parliamentary seat or the Queen's daily counsel. We are officially under the aegis of the Home Office, which is a great improvement from when we were considered a subsidiary of the army. So while I cannot contravene Brigg's decisions, I certainly can have him removed from his post, which he well knows as that's how he obtained it in the first place."

"How mercenary. And yet you look like butter wouldn't melt in your mouth."

Lear laughed again easily. "I do take enjoyment from being under-estimated."

They rode on unspeaking, the swaying of the warm carriage lulling Jaime into a semi-somnolent dream of pale clouds and dark water. He woke at Lear's touch on the back of his hand. "I was going to suggest lunch but you appear to need sleep more than anything else."

Though Jaime expected a turreted manse stuffed with carved wood and heavy old paintings, Lear's home was a fairly ordinary townhouse in Holland Park, with new furnishings and the linseed scent of recently dried paint. The walk upstairs to the guest room roused Jaime enough he bothered to disrobe, and he had just crawled between the sheets when Lear knocked lightly at the door. He entered on Jaime's word and came to the bedside.

"Is it good enough?" he asked, as if Jaime had right to complain about the sleek linens, the mountain of pillows.

"You'll fair spoil me."

Lear smiled and sat on the edge of the mattress. "Would you like to sleep? Because I can do that too."

"What do you mean?"

"Invoke a dreaming state. Send you to sleep."

"Oh. Yes. That is, if you don't mind..." Lear had already taken his hand. A leaden comfort began creeping up Jaime's arm, infiltrating his limbs and sinking him ever deeper into the mattress. His last thought before he succumbed to the loving embrace of unconsciousness was the realization that perhaps he had made a friend after all.

If Jaime dreamed, he remembered none of it. When he woke the room was dark, save for a candle flickering dully behind a pierced tin shade. He lay in bed for a little, sorting through his reluctances: to dress again in his dirty clothes, to face Lear in his own home, to confront once more the events of the day. At a knock on the door he hunched down and pulled the covers up to his chin. Nihilo entered dressed as a butler might be in crisp black, bearing a suit of clothes in his gloved hand.

"Mr Skye," he said in his soundless voice. "Given the state of your apparel, I took the liberty of removing it to be cleaned. In lieu his lordship hopes this will suffice for the evening." He hung the garments on a stand. "If you find any of the particulars unfamiliar I am at your service."

He went about lighting the wall lamps as Jaime left the bed to inspect the clothes, which consisted of a short waistcoat of dark blue silk embroidered with a spray of tiny silver stars, a tight-looking jacket in a paler blue, a white shirt and stock, and stirrupped linen trousers with a front fall rather than a centre fly. Sufficiently outdated to draw every eye were he to wear it in the street, but other than the trousers being conspicuously loose around his calves it fit him well enough. It was also the nicest suit of clothes he had ever worn, stitched by masterful hands, the linen of the shirt as soft as the bedsheets, the jacket lined in crimson silk.

Nihilo tied the starched cloth beneath Jaime's lifted chin, then conducted him to a sitting room. Adrian rose from his chair by the hearth and came to greet him. "Is it acceptable, the clothing?"

"Yes, thank you."

"It looks well on you. That is, it compliments your charms. Ah. Oh. Would you like something to drink? You don't drink. I'm going to have something to drink, though. If that's acceptable."

His face heating, Jaime nodded. Similarly flushed, Lear darted over to a small table by the curtained window where a tray stood with several decanters and a few glasses. As Lear served himself, knocking the bottle on the rim of the glass as he poured, Jaime took a seat on the firmly sprung sofa from which rose the strong scent of fresh horsehair.

"I thought your home would be, well, more like your clothes," he said for want of a topic that wasn't himself. "A bit fancier. This all looks brand new."

"It is," Lear said over his shoulder. "I'm waiting to get into my house."

"Is it under repair?"

"I don't know. It won't let me in to find out."

"The house won't let you in? Who's stopping you?"

"The house is. Ellswen is...very much not like Ordinary houses."

"Ordinary, that means not magic, doesn't it? Not like us."

"Yes, Jaime. Not like us."

With a few minutes before dinner Lear offered to show him the house. Everything was quite new and very Ordinary, at least on the surface, though Lear recommended he not look too long at the portraits on the second floor or the mirror on the landing. They ended in the library, a long room on the first floor with bookcases along one wall and a broad, baize-topped desk against the other.

"This is but a fraction of my archive," Adrian said as they strolled past the shelves. "The rest is in Ellswen." There was not a title Jaime recognized, many of them in foreign scripts, or so arcanely worded as to be in another language: *On the Orgonic Revolution of Preternatural Dynamics*, or *Shades of Mimameidr: Lesser Summonings of the Mid-*

night Clans.

"How is it you can't get into your own house?" he asked.

"Ellswen is its own possessor. Property law bends around it due to an archaic clause in the supporting papers of the Magna Carta, if I'm not mistaken."

"So then it's not your house?"

"It is part of the Lear family, and the deed to its land passes through us, but no, it is not my possession."

"And that's why it can lock you out?"

He smiled wryly. "I can't even find the gates. Apparently my grandfather neglected to tell it I was coming to stay."

"So is it like Mr Nihilo? Sometimes not all there?"

"Yes. Or rather, Mr Nihilo is like Ellswen. An avatar, if you like. Its agent in this manifested world of ours."

"I sense I'm going to have to take much of what you say on faith."

"Ask any questions you like. I've asked my share of you."

"I'm well used to being questioned. At least you aren't preparing to electrocute me or poke a syringe in my arm."

Adrian winced in sympathy. "How I wish none of that had befallen you. One liked to think, years ago, that this age would have attained a greater height of humane philosophy."

"I expect our society is only just learning how to be cruel. It takes a sophisticated mind to make another both fear death and long for it in one. And then to persuade him that the torture was all to his benefit." He shivered as a trickle of fearful sweat ran down his back, his lungs feeling pressed, his throat parched. Adrian was already reaching out to touch him and he stepped stiffly out of reach. Too many wretched memories, too many times he'd let such truths be known, only to have his pain become the other's weapon.

"Please, I must know...are we friends?"

"Of course we are, Jaime."

"But is that all you want of me?"

"For a change, it's my turn to say I don't understand."

"I've never had a friend who was ever content with only that. As I child I had no friends at all, but since then...well, no sooner have I come to trust a man than he...ruins that trust, one way or another. And I really can't bear that to happen. Not this time. So if you have any kind of amorous intentions, you'd best tell me now."

Lear couldn't look more surprised if Jaime had turned into a turnip on the spot. "Oh Jaime," he murmured, his cheeks scarlet, his voice tremulous. "I'd scarcely know what to do with them if I had."

"What do you mean?"

"If I've made you feel...put upon, that was not my desire. Want. Intention." Clutching his forehead, he swore again in his odd dialect, then cleared his throat. "Yes, I admit our friendship has swiftly grown very intimate but I shouldn't want it otherwise. That is to say, it need be no more intimate than it is already. I am quite happy as we are."

"You are?"

"I learned many years ago that a life such as mine precludes certain attachments. My longevity can be as much a curse as a blessing. It's terrible to watch people die. Worse when you love them, and you know they're asking themselves why it is you're saying goodbye."

"But why would you leave?"

He looked down, in shame or sorrow. "I could never stay until the end. Thirty, forty years of them aging and me...not? I'd break their heart."

"Saying goodbye doesn't hurt just as much?"

"Ah, but that's all at once. A single blow, rather than an erosion. Well. Let's see about that supper, shall we?"

They ate in the spacious dining room, serving themselves from dishes on a sideboard and sitting across from each other at one end of the long table. They toasted to friendship, Jaime with a glass of the gas-water Adrian had brought from Italy, the startling alkalinity of which confirmed once and for all Jaime's quiet conviction that all water had a taste.

Startling glassfuls aside, by the end of the meal Jaime was drooping in his chair and had resorted to answering Adrian's onslaught of questions about the bureaucracy of the patent office with a shrug and a grunt. They bid each other good night and Jaime returned to his room, where his cleaned and dried clothes waited atop the bureau. After carefully removing the lovely old suit and doing his best to hang it on the garment rack, he went at once to bed and slept the night through, the deep, natural sleep of anyone who'd had a difficult day and then a very pleasant meal: immobile, dreamless, at peace.

FIELD WORK

He woke early and dressed in his own clothes then made his way downstairs. Adrian was up already and waved him into the sitting room as he passed. "What do you make of this?" he asked, handing Jaime a technical drawing on a large sheet of paper. "Brigg sent it."

"Is it a pump?" Jaime asked as he followed the maze of pipes, valves, taps, gauges, each with a meticulously lettered flag describing its purported function. "It's enormous. How does it keep pressure at such volumes?"

"That's what Brigg wondered. I should like to view it in person." Jaime passed him the drawing. "Can he ask that of you?"

"No," Adrian replied absently as he inspected it again. "I want to see it for myself. I've need of a vacuum of space. This may be a useful line of inquiry." He put the paper down abruptly. "You must come along."

"Must I? I do have a job, you know."

"I'll arrange it," he said, grinning like a boy. "I'd very much like your opinions." With that he sprung from his chair and started for the door. "I've not been to the Pennines in, heavens, near on a decade. I wonder if they still make that treacle pie I like."

"Do you mean I'm to come with you?" Jaime said as he hurried after him. "Brigg will be certain there's something between us."

"Yes, a shared professional interest," Adrian replied merrily.

"But I don't know a thing about pumps."

Adrian stopped in his tracks, Jaime nearly colliding with him. "That may be so," he said. "But you know all that can be known about water."

"I don't."

He only smiled. "But you do. You just haven't remembered it yet."

There was no persuading him otherwise. Adrian was even prepared to pay Brigg for the loss of Jaime's labour, at which point Jaime relented, in the main to avoid any questions about why he was suddenly a lord's attaché. "I really ought to stop at home first," he insisted over breakfast. "These clothes aren't suitable for a journey. And please, don't offer me anything of yours. You've been very generous but it would be misplaced."

"I admit to having tastes out of fashion," Adrian said, sopping the savoury sausage grease from his plate with a bit of bread. "Plus the pantaloons don't quite fit, do they?"

"Not exactly. And there's Mrs Meldrum, she'll be worried for me."

"As you like."

They drove to Jaime's where the carriage waited at the bottom of the mews, which was too narrow to admit it. "I'd invite you in but there's nothing to see," Jaime said as he climbed down from the cab. "In fact I'm not certain we'd both fit in my room at once."

"I'm quite happy to wait." Indeed, Adrian hadn't stopped smiling since deciding on their adventure. Good to see that after a dozen decades the man still had a thirst for life.

Startled by his own acceptance of Adrian's preposterous claim, Jaime hurried to the rooming house, and was fumbling with his keyring when Mrs Meldrum yanked open the door. "Mr Skye," she said crisply as her cool gaze raked over him. "It's good to see you well."

"Ah. Yes. I was late dining at a friend's house. I didn't want to rouse you so I stayed the night."

"What manner of friend, if I may ask?"

"Oh no, it's not like that at all, Mrs Meldrum. Lord Lear is a—"

"Yes, I've met your lord," she sniffed. "Met him in your very room, I might add."

"In my room?"

"I did think you were wiser than that, Mr Skye."

"I'm...sorry?"

"As you should be. Associating with a man such as him."

"Is there something I ought to know about his lordship?"

"Nothing that isn't laid clear on the surface, for those with sense to look," she said in a scolding tone that suggested he was not among that number. "Though I'd never say so to his lordship's face. But you, Mr Skye...well I've never had cause to think poorly of you."

"Nor would I wish to give you cause. His lordship has been very friendly to me, though. I've good reason to trust him."

"Don't be fooled into thinking you can be friends with men so far above your own position. They use us to their whims and needs, and if it's ever to our benefit then it's merely by accident."

"I had no idea you held such...democratic views, Mrs Meldrum."

She lifted her chin, and her eyes, to the heavens. "It is impolite for women to discuss politics."

"Nonetheless, I admire the strength of your convictions. Good day."

He sidled past her and darted up the stairs. Here his sense of foreboding rose, coalescing around a familiar and wholly unsettling aroma, an ashy tang of spent powder and burnt sugar. Unsettling because it smelled of magic, but not Adrian's.

His room reeked of it, though there were no other signs of an intrusion. Not a thing out of place, which was easily noticed as his possessions amounted to a tin cup, a pen and inkwell, a suit and two shirts, ten books. One raincoat, badly in need of waxing. His better boots, which he did not put on, only stuffed in the bottom of his splitting case, along with the leaky raincoat and his second shirt. He put on the suit, shoved his ratty country clothes in the case, then clasped it and wrapped it with the bit of twine that kept it closed.

Reaching for the doorknob, he saw the card, lying on the floor immediately in front of the door. How could he have missed it? The scent of sugar intensified as he crouched to retrieve it. As he reached to pick it up, a shiver ran down his spine like a trickle of terror-sweat. He stood, leaving the envelope where it was.

Touch mattered to Adrian, was part of his magic. Covering his hand with his handkerchief, Jaime picked up the envelope by one corner. When nothing happened, he folded the cloth around it as best he could and shoved it in the hip pocket of his jacket, then hurried back to the carriage, where he showed it to Adrian.

"I found it in my room. It may have...arrived while I was there, for I didn't see it at first and it was right in front of the door."

"I don't think it's weighted." Adrian leaned over the card and smelled it, his nostrils flaring. "It ought to be safe to open."

"Be my guest."

"It's addressed to you, Mr Skye."

"You're the...magister."

"It may be weighted to erase itself or catch fire if opened by some-one other than the addressee."

"I thought you said it wasn't...weighted."

"I said I didn't think it was."

The envelope smelled of the other Lord Magister, but otherwise appeared entirely normal, laying on Jaime's open hand. "Ugh, all right, I'll open it. But if it does...something, you'll stop it, won't you?"

"I'll do my best."

Avoiding the seal of sluggish red wax, Jaime tore through the heavy paper and took out the folded card. The front was embossed with an arcane symbol of leaves and vines curling around a wooden chest from whence rose an open eye. Merely an engraving, but the precise execution gave the sense that the eye would blink when one's back was turned. With an angry huff, Adrian swept his hand over the card, dampening the burnt sugar smell.

"What's that symbol mean?" Jaime asked.

"I don't know."

"I don't much like hearing you say that."

"And I don't enjoy saying it."

With a flick of his wrist Jaime opened the card. The message inside was written in a startling violet ink, the more emphatic words seeming to shimmer.

To Mister J Skye IofT DofA

*Please forgive my importuning on your **esteemed** self by helping myself to discovering you, but it is with my most **humble** salutations that I would bid you welcome to our little society within our Society. Though we are Magisters all, one of your **regal** lineage ('tis true, I shall explain anon) must surely be conscious that the means of all great accomplishments are obtained by only a few.*

*When it **pleases** you to receive me, I am eager to gain your views and perchance **patronage** in a number of **lucrative** prospects which I dare to suggest will advance our shared goals of restoring the **glory** that is **England** to the **summit** of our **Craft**.*

Yours in light and plenitude,
Hercule Lorraine de la Croix Sandover, LM, IofP, BSc

"He's a liar, isn't he?" Jaime said as he held the card out for Adrian to read, for he refused to touch it.

"What makes you say so?" he asked without looking up.

"Other than him breaking into my room? Because that smell makes me sick. And this reads like the worst sort of Tory grandstanding. Awfully patriotic for a Frenchman."

"He adopted English citizenship many years ago. He's untrustworthy for other reasons."

"I've met him, you know. When I came to your club."

Adrian sat up sharply. "How?"

"On the stairs. Though I more saw than met him. Kristoff kept mum, didn't mention you at all."

"Kristoff's a gem."

"What does Sandover want, do you think?"

"Perhaps nothing," Adrian replied as Jaime put away the card. "To be able to say he was the first to meet you."

"The first after you, that is."

"Yes, I'm sure that rankles."

"Do you two not get on well?"

"He wants me dead. Have you everything you need?" Jaime only nodded. Adrian touched the roof silently and the carriage jolted into motion.

The tunnel known as the Huddersfield Narrow Canal was a marvel of engineering in its time, but strong competition from the open-water Rochdale Canal a few miles to the north and a spate of tragic drownings among the bargemen had recently put its continued operation in doubt. Shareholders in the HNC board were pressing for the canal to be enlarged, so that horses, or perhaps some novel form of pulley, might be used to ferry the barges through more efficiently than using human leggers, boatmen whose job entailed lying on their backs on planks of wood set across the bow and walking against the tunnel's low ceiling to propel the barges through, a dull, exhausting task at the best of times.

Enlarging the tunnel meant draining the canal, for which a secretive engineer had produced a prototype of a new form of steam-driven pump. Two pumps as it turned out, one upstream, one down. Between them was the mountain, and a pair of very, very long pipes running the length of the tunnel, transmitting under pressure the water which otherwise would fill the lower half. There was a great deal more, about rates of flow and circumferences of pipes and valves, which might have made excellent sense were Jaime at his desk with the blueprints to hand and not in a first class carriage on a swaying northbound train being lectured by an effervescent Adrian.

They were the only passengers in the carriage, Adrian having reserved it entire, a stunning show of the wealth at which he had only hinted. Jaime soon fell asleep, soothed by the muted atmosphere and cushioned benches, and sore of head from all he was being asked to believe.

He woke as they were approaching London Road Station, where they changed to a smaller, smellier engine which took them east from Manchester to Oldfield. To reach Diggle, the village where the canal tunnel emerged, Adrian hired a man with a cart. A figure of complete normalcy, the man neither smoked nor spoke, his clothes patched but decent, his cart a plain wooden box on a pair of axels, the horse a middling brown gelding which never changed its reliable yet unhurried gait up the curving Huddersfield Road.

Seated on a pair of crates, their backs to the driver, they took turns playing at Adrian's trick of filling one's hand with water, though Jaime could no more than break a sweat on his upturned palm. "You're thinking too concretely," Adrian said under the clop of hooves and creak of cart. "Trust that it will give you what you want."

"But what's *it*? Who's doing the giving?"

"Whoever gives the weather," he said with a grin. "We say it's raining as if that's a grammatically coherent sentence, but who or what is the *it*?"

"So it's best to think of it as weather, you mean?"

"It's analogous, yes. Only very, very localized."

Weather, which came from everywhere and nowhere, which was a general feature of a turning planet. A watery planet, his own cells flooded with it, his life dependent on it, as was all other known life. Inevitably, as the tides, as the rain, the moisture beaded his palm, and for the first time in years, he raised his hand and tasted...not salt, not sweat, but water, pure and clear.

"I wish I understood," he said half to himself.

"So do I," Adrian said wryly.

"You mean you don't?"

"Water-work is surprisingly opaque to inquiry. We know it appears matrilineally, passing from mother to daughter, save in those cases where there is no daughter. Does...sorry, did your father have siblings?"

"None I knew of."

"Then it came to you through him, and he through his mother, Mammy Skye."

"How is it you know she's alive?" Jaime asked, for he'd been told time and again he had no kinfolk, that there'd been no one to claim him.

"I visit with her now and then."

"You visit with my grandmother?"

"I visit with Mammy Skye, one of the most powerful witches I've ever known."

"If you say so."

"I can take you to see her if you like."

Jaime had no reply. He'd been but an infant when orphaned. Had no recollection of another family member's face. She would be a stranger. A stranger who knew all about him. His closest living kin. His kin who hadn't wanted him.

Adrian was sitting very still, with a look of immense concentration. "There," he said suddenly, one finger raised. "Do you hear that?"

"What am I listening for?"

He was about to reply then caught himself and smiled. "I should like to know if you can discern it for yourself."

The air was awash in sound: the wheels on the gritted road, the fall of the horse's hooves, the squeak of wood against wood. The breeze through the leaves and the birds on the branches, his own heartbeat, his breath. The sounds of any country scene, completed by the ping of a blacksmith's hammer as they rounded the last hill before Diggle. The forge must be nearby, for it seemed he could hear its furnace. Smell it even, though it struck his nose differently than a smithy. A bitter, clinging, smoky scent atop the usual smells of dung and earth and self.

"What is that awful smell?"

"I believe it's what we're here to investigate."

Diggle was a well-settled village along the canal's western bank, with numerous two-storey warehouses of sandy brick clustered around the lock, which was presently closed. A few hundred yards up the canal sat the machine, mounted directly over the opening of the tunnel and rising from the murky water like the segmented carapace of some extinct aquatic beast. A steady stream of water gushed from a wide outlet on its back just above the surface. The coal gas-driven engine sat on the shore beside, hissing steam and the smoke which was the source of the unpleasant odour.

The noise was unreal, dominating the valley with a buzzing, clanking drone interspersed with the occasional hiss of a vent. Everyone had raised their voices to compensate and the dockyard bristled with discordant energy, the waterway jammed up with all manner of barges and smaller vessels caught in the bottleneck of cargo caused by the canal's unexpected closure. Meanwhile the machine kept chugging, the workmen clustered nearby seeming to have no task but to stand there and watch it do so.

"It's a shame Pickford isn't seeing this," Jaime half shouted in Adrian's ear as they approached the engine. "He loves great big things."

"Curious. Brigg didn't bat an eye when I told him I wanted you instead."

"That is curious. Him and Pickford are thick as thieves."

A stocky man with the salt-and-pepper hair, stern brow, and comparatively clean overalls of a foreman came to meet them. He and Adrian exchanged a few words that Jaime's ears missed amid the crush of sound. He then gestured to one of the workers, who nodded then climbed a ladder of metal rungs on the side of the pump's oily shell to open a hatch on the top.

"Do you mean to go inside that thing?" Jaime shouted to Adrian.

Adrian was tucking his frilled shirt cuffs inside his jacket sleeves, readying himself for the descent. "You're welcome to wait out here," he replied easily, his voice carrying in that unnatural way.

Alone. For possibly hours. while the workmen either hostilely ignored him or, even worse, attempted to make conversation. All because he was timid. "I'll come."

It helped that the foreman descended first, bearing a bright lantern. Then Adrian, equipped with same, the white stone of his illuminating brooch quiescent and dull. Jaime last, descending into the uneven sphere of light around the lanterns and the pair of gas lamps fixed to the walls of the tunnel.

This face of the machine was less complex than the outer shell, merely iron plating from which emerged a pair of pipes, each nearly a foot in diameter. The pipes lead away into the absolute darkness of the tunnel. "Now, you'll want to be ignoring any bones or such you come across," the foreman shouted, for the noise of the engine was hardly diminished.

"What do you mean, bones?" Jaime cried, but if his terror was apparent the foreman gave it no thought.

"Well now, it's been a good forty years this canal's been operating," he went on. "Now and then...well, one don't always have a way to find them that's lost."

"How lost could one get in a tunnel?" Adrian asked.

The foreman's face hardened and he lowered his gaze. "He means drowned," Jaime replied. "That's what you mean, isn't it?"

"Leggers know their trade," the foreman replied gruffly. "They know the risks."

"This is why we're here, Jaime," Adrian said in his softly carrying voice. "To see if conditions can't be improved, lives saved. Thank you, Mr Wise. We'll mind ourselves from here."

"As you like. And don't mind anything strange you hear. The way the wind carries down the air shafts can put a body in a terrible fear, but I don't put no stock in ghosts and neither ought you, sirs." With this he departed, taking his lantern though Jaime had hoped he would leave it.

"Now what?" he yelled to Adrian who was holding up the other lantern to more closely inspect the shuddering machine.

"Now we visit the operations at the intake," he replied. "I lack confidence in the volumes our engineer Mr Czerny purports to be able to move."

"You mean we've got to go to the other end?"

"It shouldn't take us more than an hour to walk the three miles. It's very level terrain, obviously."

"Three miles? Through there?" He pointed down the tunnel stretching blackly away, what little they could see of its walls slimed with decades of moss and muck.

"Why should we not?"

Because it looked like a catacomb or a gateway to hell. Because there was something in the air he didn't like but couldn't name. Adrian was unaffected, blithe as in the meadow, and he was twenty yards away already and taking the light with him. Cringing at the sound of his breath and footsteps echoing off the arched ceiling of crumbling brick, Jaime ran to catch up.

After a while they reached a place where the roof was no longer bricks but bare rock. On they went, and on, and nowhere to go but on, and all the while he fought a terrible urge to look behind him, but what would he see? The same as what was before him: nothing whatsoever but slimy rock and a cold infinity. Adrian had gotten a few steps ahead, his dark hair indistinct from the darkness everywhere, until Jaime began to fear that when the man turned he would hardly be there at all, would reveal not that boyish grin but a faceless void like his servant Nihilo.

They had to be near the middle of the tunnel, beneath the summit of the hill, its gargantuan bulk suspended above them by no more than inertia and a thin shell of human endeavour. Were they descending even deeper? Impossible, or else it wouldn't serve as a canal, but he could swear the tunnel floor sloped downwards, leading them ever farther from the realm of light and hope.

His feet slowed, then stopped. Adrian turned, the glow from his strange brooch lighting his face grotesquely from below. "What's wrong?"

"It's nothing."

"Don't deny your fears, Jaime. They usually mean something."

"I just don't like being this penned in. It feels dead down here."

"I know. I don't like it either."

"Shouldn't there be adjoining shafts? There's a rail line running parallel, no?"

"There is. We just passed a point of access. And we are now at the approximate middle of the tunnel. It will take as long to return as it will to go on."

Returning meant turning his back on his foreboding. "Might as well keep on, then. Be done with it."

"Is that what you want?"

"I want to be in your sitting room with a cup of tea, if you must know."

"So do I. This is not nearly so interesting as I wished."

"Let's go." Easier to say than do, for his feet had turned to clay.

"Take my hand," Adrian said, reaching for him.

"I'm not a child."

"No. You're my good friend and we're doing something possibly very dangerous. Let's share our strengths. You've nothing to prove to me."

"How dangerous?"

"I don't know."

"I hate when you say that."

"Would you rather I lie to you?" He was still holding out his hand, his expression mild, save for his eyes, which seemed nearly to glow, the green gone to icy blue.

"No. No, I'd rather know we're both lost."

"It's a straight line. We can't possibly get lost."

"You know what I mean."

"I do. Please excuse my irreverence."

"No apology needed. We could do with some levity." His fears fading, Jaime took his first deep breath of many minutes. Smelled burnt sugar. "Sandover..." he murmured, the aroma unmistakeable though it was impossible the man was near.

"What did you say?" Adrian's smile had vanished, his eyes darkening by the second.

"It smells just like him."

For a long moment Adrian only stared, the stone of his brooch flickering rapidly. He looked down the tunnel, licked his lips. "We need to leave at once."

Jaime followed Adrian's gaze and felt it, a great weight pushing towards him, like an immense wave. A fetid breeze slithered past with a hollow whisper, tasting of death.

"Agreed." He took Adrian's hand firmly and they began walking back the way they had come. The danger was near, was real and very near and getting nearer, the massive pipes running down the centre of the tunnel seeming to vibrate with their passing steps.

"Don't let go of my hand," Adrian said with a glance at the humming pipes. "But I think we ought to run."

"Agreed." And they did, Jaime gripping Adrian's hand like a lifeline, pursued by a growing sound, a terrible thrumming of the rank air, in symphony with the rattle of the pipes as they began to clatter against the rocky ground.

There was a curious pinging from behind, the sound of a small piece of metal hitting rock at high speed, followed by a sickening whiff of Sandover's magic. There was another pinging, then another, as the smell of dank water rose beneath the bittersweetness. Jaime's lungs ached, and his legs, and his feet from striking stone. Still they ran, as the first rivulets of water snaked along the cracks, as the rivulets overspilled their narrow banks and became puddles, as the puddles merged and became a sheet of flowing water. Water which kept rising.

"Why is this happening?" Jaime gasped as the water clutched at his feet, slowing their steps like in some ghastly dream.

"I told you he wants me dead. And he knows you'll survive."

"But aren't you immortal?"

"Thankfully no. But this is far too soon to pass the veil."

Making a flicking motion with his crooked left hand at the surging water in their path, Adrian spat a slithering word that set Jaime's teeth on edge. The water before them split as if in the wake of a fast ship, leaving a path of clear if wet stone down which they now ran at all speed. Still came the water, rising to either side of them until it was nearly to their waists, the path between the two standing waves growing narrower and narrower.

"We must stop the flood," Adrian shouted.

"The machine at the end will stop it. Won't it?"

"This much pressure? Driven by craft? That thing will be blown like a cork straight out of the tunnel and into the lock."

"It'll smash everything! The workers, the town..."

"Most likely."

"What are we meant to do? There's no chance we'll outrace this!"

"I know." He stopped and spun about, throwing up both hands as he spoke another string of unearthly syllables that sucked the breath from Jaime's lungs like a winter's gale.

The roar of onrushing water was damped by a horrific cracking sound, like an ice-bound lake in a sudden thaw. Without Adrian's interference, the standing waves had broken over the temporary path, and the water surging round Jaime's knees was suddenly frigid, a bone-deep, murderous cold that made him cry out, his feet feeling dipped in fire.

Adrian cursed in his ancient words. "Sorry," he added as he waded towards Jaime. And then swore again as a piece of flotsam struck his leg. He cast an angry gesture at the object, which broke apart with the same cracking sound.

"T-t-t-t-too c-c-c-c-cold..."

"Sorry, sorry..."

Blessed warmth flooded Jaime's rigid body. His muscles shrieking, he grabbed for Adrian's hand, the skin contact accelerating the flow of power. "Why did you do that?"

"Calculated risk. I hoped not to affect you."

A gust of hot wind whistled overhead, stirring their hair and clothes and carrying the smell of sugared pitch. From the depths of the tunnel came another immense cracking, as if the world were breaking in half, then the sickening roar of a river in spate as a waist-high wave came frothing towards them, laden with hunks of ice the size of hams.

His face contorted with uncanny rage, Adrian smashed his hands together then flung his gathered forces at the wave, which vaporized in a blast of impossible light, sending shards of ice flying. "Shield your eyes," he cried over his shoulder, then did it again, setting the tunnel ablaze, the grimy bricks and blackened stone bleached to white.

Dazzled, half blinded, Jaime flung his arm over his face. Reeking of gun-smoke, another gust of rearward wind went ripping past, striking Jaime like a kick in the back and knocking him flat. For terrible seconds he floundered face down in the icy water, until his fingertips scraped rock. He bent his knees, met solid ground. When he raised his head, Adrian was gone.

UNDERHILL

Crouching on all fours in a foot of frigid water, soaked to the bone and shivering so hard he could scarcely breathe, his only light a wavering dimness far down the tunnel, completely alone: every nightmare there was, all at once and real. Yet if this was truly a nightmare where were his hospital bed and the hypodermic? The white walls with their staring faces? In which case this really was his life, and this was how it ended.

If he surrendered. If he let this be his end. Just when he'd been granted a new beginning, by the only person who had ever told him the truth. Who at this very moment was trading his unceasing life for the safety of one hillside village.

If only he wasn't so cold. If he weren't cold, he could move. If he were dry, he'd not be cold. Adrian had words aplenty for what it was he did when he did what he did, but wasn't it foremost an act of will?

Off...get off...every drip...evaporate, boil, succumb, be off be off be off...

His eyes closed, he was nearly knocked down again as a drifting lump of ice bashed into his arms. He had to stand, get free of the water, though it had stopped rising. He let its current push him back on his heels. Either his eyes were failing or the light was growing dimmer, the fear of losing it entirely what drove him to his feet.

Off, off, be off, be dry. Perhaps it was working as the searing pinch of cold began to relinquish its hold on his spine. He took a step forward, then another, whispering the words until they felt like a spell, his gaze pinned to the trembling light, the water dragging at his sodden shoes.

The worst that might happen was he shouted at water. The best was that it worked. "Away from me! Away, I said!"

Perhaps it rippled but it wasn't enough, no matter how he waved his hands, how hard he wished. Of all the times for his curse to desert him, as another foul gust of hot wind raked over him, stinking of sugar, the ice flowing past Jaime's legs splintering in the sudden thaw. "Damn you, Sandover, I'll not lose him to you! *Away!*"

In fury, in need, in a blind faith in the unseen, he stamped his foot as if he was stamping on Sandover's arrogant face. Like he'd hurled a boulder the water sprayed out in a bowl, striking the sides of the tunnel hard and raining back down upon him. With a wild hoot of laughter he did it again, for the stunning delight, for the raw sense of power. Then with the water fleeing from his every step, he ran towards the light.

The light which grew and grew, as bright as the sun and as cold as the moon, a shining curtain of impossible light like that which had blocked the rain on the heath but ten times the strength, so bright Jaime could barely make out Adrian's slender silhouette at its blazing heart.

Thigh-deep in the frigid water, both hands up before him, he was leaned into his spell like a man trying to push a boulder uphill. Or hold back a river, for still the water came, filling the tunnel to the roof and forcing itself around Adrian's obstruction, pouring even over the top to meet again in a churning current that was half waterfall, half sucking maelstrom.

The smell of Sandover was everywhere, and the smell of the magisters' craft in action, as if the air was on fire. And all of it real, not a nightmare or a drug's effect or a madman's ravings but the truth. If so, the truth was that Jaime had a duty to help this extraordinary man, this man he should never have met, who had given him back his life.

"What can I do?" Jaime shouted, squinting through his fanned fingers as he waded towards him.

"Hands!" Adrian cried, and never had his voice sounded more human, ragged and full of fear. "I need your hands on me."

"Where?"

"Anywhere! Please, Jaime..."

"Is this—"

He needn't question if it was working, for his hand had already welded itself to Adrian's shoulder, a penetrating contact as if he weren't feeling the wet, torn cloth of Adrian's jacket but his bare skin. Deeper, down through sinew and muscle to touch his very bones, the power flowing back and forth between them in an accelerating circuit. The light was extraordinary, yet Jaime's eyes no longer ached, each cresting wave as it hurtled towards them revealing itself with the intricacy of an engraving. Adrian was breathing hard but had stopped trembling, and dared a glance back.

"Thank the gods you're here. I so hated to leave you."

"You did what you had to. Now how do we stop this?"

"We've got to empty the tunnel. But I can't just want it away. We know nothing of the terrain. It could flood Diggle, the farms, do all the harm we're trying to prevent."

"Then where?"

"I don't know!"

"Stop saying that!"

Adrian choked out a bitter laugh. "I'm so sorry, Jaime. It was I who brought you into this disaster."

"I was already a disaster. You made me whole again."

He laughed again then cried out, not in pain but in wonder. "The sky," he gasped.

"Yes, like the sky."

"No, Jaime, I mean use it! Make clouds."

"In the tunnel?"

"In the sky."

"How? I can't see the sky."

"You don't need to see it, you are it! You are clouds and the wind that bears them. Waves and the sea that births them. Be who you are, Jaime!"

"Air," he cried as the gears of his mechanical mind clicked into place.

"No, water," Adrian shouted back frantically.

"No, air, an air shaft. That's where it can go."

"But you don't need—"

"Shut up! I'm working." Be off be off be gone! Be clouds and boil away into beyond. Go water a swamp, for all I care. Be gone be off be gone!

And all the while he compelled himself to see it, as clear as day, as the truth, envisioning the water as it leaped and boiled itself into long plumes of no account, fighting itself in its urgency to escape Sandover's spell. The water wanted to be free. "There's vents all along the tunnel!" he shouted, as if the water could hear him, but who had ever said it couldn't? Only the liars. "Go! Go now! Away with you!"

"Whatever you're doing, don't stop," Adrian croaked. He was shaking again, rivulets of steam rising from his hands which had shrivelled to claws.

"I don't mean his water!" Jamie cried. "Sorry, sorry…"

"Forget me. Do what you must."

Protect you. Destroy Sandover. Ruining his vile endeavour was a good place to start. Be off and be gone and take his murderous machines apart as you go! GO!

All the air seemed to disappear from the tunnel in a single sucking gust that tore at their clothes and hair as it raced past, distorting Adrian's illuminated plane into a punctured cone, like Jaime had hurled a spear, the water around them boiling without heat into an icy fog so thick Adrian disappeared. Then did the world.

His first thought on waking was crushingly familiar. The second much less, for instead of a sharp-faced nurse or a bespectacled doctor waiting for him to rouse from his stupor, the person seated in the chair beside his hospital bed was Adrian. Surely it was him, though his head was lowered. No one else had that sort of green jacket, or might be wearing it with bleached buckskins, leaning back with one booted ankle hooked over his other knee, his nose in a little blue book like he sat fireside in the magisters' club and not on a cheap wooden stool in a hospital room that stank like all hospital rooms of vinegar and hopelessness.

Jaime opened his mouth but no sound emerged but a breathy whimper. He hurt from head to toe, with the penetrating ache that followed a vigorous course of hydrotherapy, as if he'd been held under a waterfall while being beaten with planks. He licked his lips, that itself an effort, then tried again. "I'm dead, aren't I?"

"Not in the slightest," Adrian replied with a smile as he closed his book. "But I wouldn't try to sit up."

"I feel dead."

"I don't believe the dead can feel. So that's your first piece of evidence that you aren't among their number."

"Shut up…"

When he woke again night had fallen, for the curtains were closed and a shaded candle burned on the bedside table. He gazed at it for some time before noticing Adrian at the edge of its meagre glow. Sitting on the floor with his eyes closed, his legs bent and crossed, his hands soft on his knees, he appeared to be sleeping, though the moment Jaime stirred he opened his eyes.

"Do you feel alive yet?" he asked quietly.

"I'd ask you the same," Jaime rasped. "Were you asleep?"

"Asleep enough." He rose and stretched his limbs, then drew the stool nearer the bedside. He looked if not his age then certainly worn, his fine clothes creased, his eyes deeply shadowed.

"You didn't need to sit vigil," Jaime said.

"I did. If only for the good of my soul. You see? I'm as selfish as I ever was."

"If you say so."

He laughed a little, no more than a hard breath and a wry smile. "Thank you for coming to my aid."

"I'm guessing it worked, then."

He laughed again with more humour. "Yes, or else I'd not be here for you to ask. I have had to invent some quite interesting explanations for why several thousand cubic yards of cold steam came shooting from the hillside."

"Who put you in charge of explaining that?"

"I did. There's a very robust inquiry being made by the union of engineers and the canal firm's board of directors. Apparently no one knows who authorized the trial of the pumps."

"Why can't they ask the engineer, Czerny?"

"Because he's dead."

"He's what?" He lurched upright, sick with shock. "Why didn't you tell me?"

"It wasn't your doing, Jaime. They found him in his home. It's been recorded as a suicide."

"But you don't think it was, do you?"

Adrian made a bitter face. "Not unless someone has devised a means of immolating his own body in bed without so much as scorching the sheets."

"How can he get away with it?" There was no need to name the man. "Don't your lot have some sort of...I don't know, rules? Surely you can't just go about breaking the law."

"Yes, we have rules, and no, one cannot flout English or any other law simply by being a magister. But our—my—opponent has thus far evaded any direct blame. Through proxies, or blackmail, however he can achieve it. Though I am beginning to suspect he has a patron of his own."

"He's a murderer."

"I'm afraid so."

They sat without speaking, not a sound breaking the twilit silence of the hospital, the shaded candle casting Adrian's ancient, ageless face in bronze, a mask concealing a century of sorrow. Jaime placed his hand softly over Adrian's where it lay on the coverlet, and wished with everything he had for happiness, some glimmer of joy to lighten their hearts, soothe the lingering hurts of having faced death. And maybe it worked, or perhaps it was just the gift of touch, as Adrian's stark expression softened to a gentle smile.

"I think I'd like to sleep again," Jaime said. "Can you…"

"Of course." Adrian laid his other hand over Jaime's. "Now that I know you're well, I also can rest."

Jaime wanted to reply, chide him again for suffering while Jaime lolled in bed, but there was no good telling Adrian what to do. Besides, he was already dissolving in a haze of golden light as Jaime fell asleep. Though it felt less like falling and more like taking flight.

AN UNFORESEEN DEPARTURE

He was not at all injured, his collapse due to exhaustion, which Adrian explained was quite a common occurrence among young or untrained craftspeople after their first major working. They returned to London the following day, where Jaime insisted on introducing Adrian to Mrs Meldrum, who was first much chastened by having thought wrongly of Jaime, and then incensed that anyone should have entered her home without her leave, making of her yet another enemy for Sandover.

Far more confronting was their next visit. Arbitration Hall was a graceless ivy-swathed stone building on the edge of Ladbroke Square, and housed the bodies responsible for investigating and bringing to justice crimes of craft. What Jaime had done in Diggle was not a crime as such, but it had encouraged a great deal of Ordinary attention to the crafting world, for which they were now expected to account.

In a stuffy, high-ceilinged room like that in many a sanatorium they sat before a panel of three of Adrian's frowning peers who like any board of hospital adjudicators spoke of Jaime with immense authority without once speaking *to* him, until Adrian curtly ended the interview and ushered him out of the room.

"Thank you," Jaime said once they were in the corridor. "For getting me out of there, that is."

"Really? I was about to apologize for subjecting you to this."

"To be fair, I thought they'd show you more respect."

"Trust me when I say their disrespect is well earned. Will you come to dinner?"

He ought to accept. Take every kindness granted, for all that he'd had so little of it. "I'm sorry," he found himself saying. "I think once again what I most need is sleep. And before you offer, I mean in my own bed." In his own quiet room, free from faceless men and dangerous paintings and Adrian himself, endlessly astonishing, the least ordinary man Jaime had ever known.

"I understand," Adrian said with a sad little smile and the barest hitch in his voice. "And please do promise me you'll be gentle with yourself for a while."

"As gentle as Brigg will allow. I've been off work for days."

"I'll write to him. He'll take it from me."

The sun was dropping beneath the inevitable blanket of city smoke as they descended the front steps of Arbitration House, long spears of russet light catching in the leaves of the trees on the park and outlining Adrian's dark head in gleaming gold.

"Until next we meet, Lord Lear," Jaime said, offering his hand.

"I remain at your most humble service, Mr Skye," Adrian replied as they shook. And then he was gone, that most extraordinary of men, whistling an old country tune as he set off across the shadowy park, stepping on the fallen lilac blossoms which lay along the dark pathway like stars.

Happily numb, Jaime was nearly home before he smelled the person following him. He stopped under the next lamp and turned, expecting Sandover and not a young man dressed like he'd stepped out of a French tailor's look-book.

"I beg your pardon, Mr Skye," the pretty man said, removing his cocked hat to reveal a head of artful black curls. "I don't mean to intrude—"

"Yet here you are doing just that. Who are you and what do you want?"

"My master very badly wishes to meet you, Mr Skye," he replied sweetly.

"If your master is who I imagine, I'll not hear another word from you."

"It's a pity that you've been given the wrong impression," he said through his pearly teeth.

"My impression is my own. I'll thank you and your master to leave me be." He started walking again but the sickening smell pursued him swifter than even the young man's footsteps. His head was pounding, the exertions of the day weighing on him, dragging at his legs like that wretched water, until every step was an agony. His last thought as he fell was that he ought to have had dinner with Adrian after all.

Water woke him. Water in immense volumes, water that knew him and wanted him to wake. He could smell it all around him, water and rotting wood and tar and canvas and salt and the dung of cart horses, each breath painting incandescent pictures in his reeling mind. With the smells came the noise, of shouting men and bellowing steers and the repetitive clang of a bell, and beneath these the ceaseless plip and ripple of water against the hulls of many ships. As boots thudded towards him he stopped trying to open his leaden eyes.

"We meant to carry 'im like that?" a man grunted.

"'e ain't in no shape to walk, is 'e?" came the slurring reply.

"Give 'im the boot, that'll shape 'im up," said a third.

"That's your answer to everything," the first spat. "Just pick an end and get on. Tide's going out and we're going with."

Not if Jaime had the say of it. Yet his aching limbs refused to answer his directives, remaining limp and unresisting as the rogues hoisted him between them like a sack of grain and started up the gangplank.

Don't let them take me...

He was suddenly pitched to the side as the gangplank tilted wildly, the cries of the sailors and wharf-men growing panicked as a freakish wave rocked every craft in the harbour. His arse struck wood as the men let him go, the impact jarring him properly awake. They hadn't bothered to tie him, and with the rattish instincts of a man who'd grown up poor, slim, and strange, he flung himself onto his front and squirmed between the bowed legs of the fellow in his way, who was busy clinging to the rope rails of the swaying gangplank.

If not for fear of being crushed against the stone jetty by the yawing ship he might have pitched himself straight into the oily water below, for nothing could drown him. Instead he scrambled to his feet and made a dash for dry land, ignoring the shouts behind him, the mad clanging of bells and men yelling from the rigging as another huge wave slammed into the harbour.

He caught scent of the sickly char of Sandover's magic amid the fuzz of dockyard odours. What a fool he'd been to think himself safe from a man of such malevolence. There was only one place in the world he was safe, and it was with—

His head seemed to burst, pain lancing down his spine as someone grabbed him by the hair, his agonized shriek dying to a feeble wheeze as a huge brown arm clamped around his middle and crushed the breath from his lungs. Still he fought, until the beast let go of Jaime's hair to thump him on the back of the head.

"Quit squirming, you ratbag," he grunted, hoisting Jaime clear off his feet.

Black pain swamping his vision, he sagged in his captor's crushing grip, but at the thud of the man's heavy boots on the hollow deck of the ship he roused in a desperate fit of kicking and thrashing. Put to rest as the beast slammed him bodily against the side of the cabin. Held him there with one enormous hand against his throat.

Six feet or more if he was an inch, the man was broad as a church door, with a square chin and a thunderous brow beneath which shone eyes of a startling blue. Eyes which held Jaime as firmly as the man's cruel grip, stripping away his last hope of liberty.

"Get on with it then," he choked. "Whatever it is you're going to do to me."

The man's brows drew together, his eyes like shards of deadly ice. He licked his lips, drew breath as if to speak. Sighed heavily, then yanked open a door beside Jaime and shoved him through it.

He fetched up against a wall almost at once. Turned in time to see the cabin door close. The man locked it from outside and walked away, leaving Jaime in darkness. He ought to feel about the room, assess his circumstances, learn what he could of his fate, but what good could it do? Sandover had him, that much was clear from the persistent stink. And Adrian might never know.

Don't let them take me...

Perhaps Sandover's magic was damping his own, as he wished and wished and wished in vain for all the world's water to rise up, smash the ship apart, set him free. Wished until he was speaking the words aloud, then screaming them, then whispering again as his voice gave out, alone in the dark, his clothes drenched with fear, his heart in pieces, his hope destroyed.

Tears followed. As did the rain.

to be continued...

Who does Sandover serve, and why does
he want Adrian dead? Learn the truth in
The Deathless Duke: Elsewhen Book 1
coming in 2024

There's something dreadful at the bottom of the lake.
Jaime Skye is going down to meet it.
Whether he wants to or not.

Skye's Fall: Book 1 of the Jaime Skye Chronicles
Monsters, myths, and magic collide in this Achillean Ace/Aro
Gaslamp Fantasy tale

Join the Readers Club for free books and news about these and other
exciting releases!
www.willforrest.com/newsletter/

THANKS

Many thanks to...

Marie Mckay, whose enthusiasm for this story gave me the confidence to make it a series.

Dave Chesson, whose site Kindlepreneur.com is a bottomless well of things to help authors and who knows some dang things about formatting a book.

Clan Sharkey, for sushi and succour.

Clan Forrest, for love.

About the Author

Author, blogger, and general nuisance Will Forrest (they/them) writes unusual (and usually queer) Historical and Paranormal Romances with a dash of mischief and mayhem. Will grew up on a steady diet of Douglas Adams and classic 90s bodice rippers, and has a diploma of fashion design, a degree in social theory, and a bad habit of changing careers, life goals, and continents. Currently Will lives in a very warm part of Canada with three lovely humans and a succession of martyred houseplants.

Join the Readers Club for advance access, free books, and (occasionally) recipes.

www.willforrest.com

ALSO BY WILL FORREST

THE OLD RAZZLE DAZZLE: a London Hustle book

Two romances, two eras & too much drama when an aging theatre director becomes the unlikely mentor to a talented young singer in this Edwardian-era novel of loss and redemption.
"An R-rated queer historical Hallmark romance" (Britt Hanowell, Boundless Words)

AN INCONVENIENT EARL: a Gay Regency Romance

A passionate tale of freedom, forgiveness, and saying exactly the wrong thing in bed.

www.willforrest.com